TY D SITES
Who stole the surveyor's lunch?

Dedication

To Stephen Pycroft, a stalwart of the construction industry, who is bowing out this year after an illustrious career. Recently dubbed 'The Godfather' by Building Magazine, he has not only made a massive contribution to the industry and led his own organisation to meteoric success, but has made a crucial contribution to the success of many smaller construction companies.

Stephen and his late wife, Joanne, formed a firm friendship with my parents and were a huge support in helping them establishing their small construction business back in the 80s and 90s. His mentoring has played a key role in my own personal development within the industry over the years too, for which I'll be eternally grateful.
SSD

Foreword

During my career in construction, The Shard has to be the project that I am most proud of; one that changed the course of the company and placing it on an upward trajectory. We had a great team on the project which engendered a unique and collaborative culture working together - from the client to the consultants and trades on site. A number of great stories came out of the construction of the Shard but, without giving away the story here, the incident on which this story is based was definitely memorable and made it on to the mainstream news and into the papers.

The book portrays a number of interesting and important roles and trades that you find on every construction site, particularly quantity surveyors, which is where I started my career in the industry. It's great to see the diversity and inclusion portrayed throughout the book, particularly with the message on the final page where everyone comes together and where I also have a cameo of my own!

I have known Saheb since he was a young child, and I have watched him develop into the person he has become over recent years. It gives me great pride to see the positive contributions he is making within the construction industry and the award winning success the previous Ty D Sites book has achieved.

I hope this book shows children and their parents how there are many interesting and varied roles and trades within the construction industry and how every day on a construction site can throw up a different surprise.

Stephen Pycroft
Group Chairman, Mace Group

One beautiful day with the sun on display,
A bright blue sky not a speckle of grey.

The site is unlocked in the morning by Saad,
Security guard says "Welcome to The Shard."

All people line up and they wait to go in,
They tap on the turnstiles and give it a spin.

"Good morning" and "Hi" they are greeted by Ty,
With Dana and John who are helping nearby.

Date : _____ Project No :_____

Project Name : _____

DGP Logistics

DAY	JOB DESCRIPTION	IN	OUT
MONDAY		07.00	17.00
TUESDAY		07.00	17.00
WEDNESDAY		07.00	17.00
THURSDAY		07.00	17.00
FRIDAY			
SATURDAY			
SUNDAY			

"Good morning Miss Hayer" they greet the surveyor,
She's always too cold wearing layer on layer.

But she is the one you would say is the payer,
So any request or command just obey her!

She asks them to send a report to her fast,
That shows what the time was when workers went past.

She checks when they came and she checks when they went,
She adds all the hours on site that they spent.

TOTAL HOURS

Logistics Manager :

Sign : _____ Print : _____ Date : _____

Client :

Sign : _____ Print : _____ Date : _____

QUOTATION

SCOPE	QTY	PRICE	TOTAL
1			
2 Surveyors all sit in the office together, They work as a team and like birds of a feather.			
3 They tap and they tap all the keys on the board, To see what the costs are, what they can afford.			
4 They add all the bills from the builders and all, They make the agreements and set out their stall.			
5 At maths they are good with the numbers they crunch, But never so good when you ask them for lunch!			
6			
7			
8			
9			
		TOTAL	

The thought of her lunch got her tummy to rumble,
The apple, the rice and the strawberry crumble.

Her mummy had made her a curry with rice,
Perfecting the salt and the level of spice.

She looks for her bag and she sees it's not there,
Did somebody take it? But no one would dare!

And then she remembered where it was last seen,
She left it beside the new vending machine.

She went to go check whether it was still there,
But no it was not as the floor was all clear.

As Saad could detect her distress and dismay,
He offered to help and assist any way.

She asked if he saw who had taken her food,
And who it could be that would mess up her mood.

"Although I have not but let's give it a shot,
The camera footage can tell us a lot."

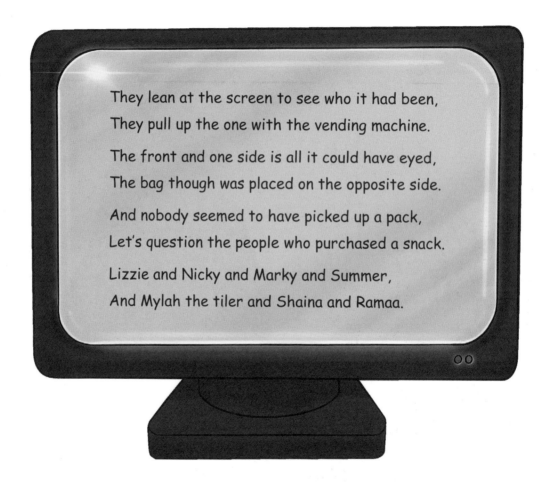

They lean at the screen to see who it had been,
They pull up the one with the vending machine.

The front and one side is all it could have eyed,
The bag though was placed on the opposite side.

And nobody seemed to have picked up a pack,
Let's question the people who purchased a snack.

Lizzie and Nicky and Marky and Summer,
And Mylah the tiler and Shaina and Ramaa.

Elizabeth Hecht who is Chief Architect,
Her job is to draw up and dream the project.

Select or reject each object to be specced,
Then she will inspect what the builders erect.

"Good morning Miss Hecht, you are not a suspect,
With all due respect may we ask you direct?

Just who stole her lunch as her day has been wrecked?"
"No sorry, I just seem to not recollect."

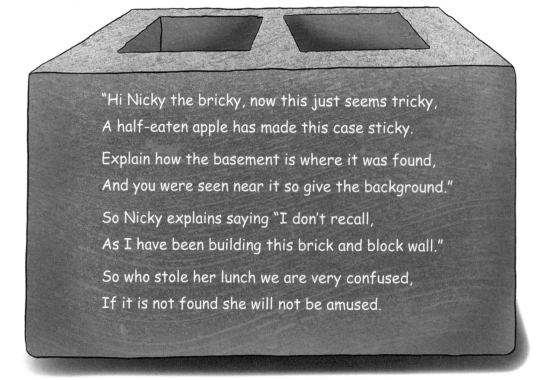

"Hi Nicky the bricky, now this just seems tricky,
A half-eaten apple has made this case sticky.

Explain how the basement is where it was found,
And you were seen near it so give the background."

So Nicky explains saying "I don't recall,
As I have been building this brick and block wall."

So who stole her lunch we are very confused,
If it is not found she will not be amused.

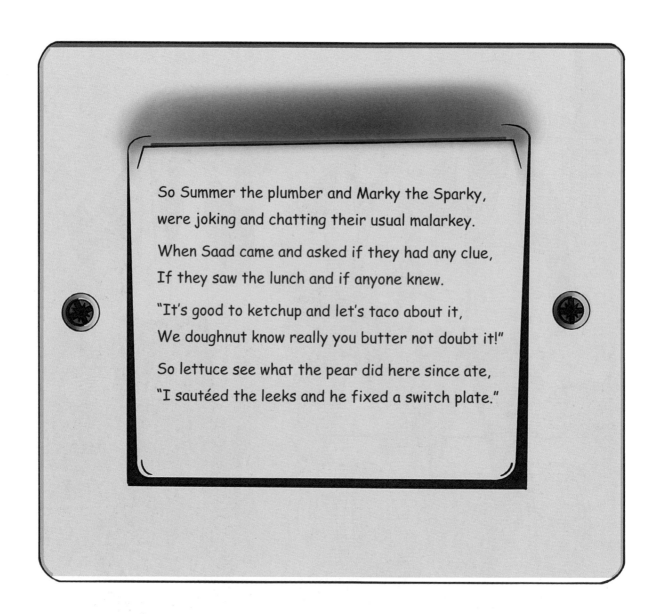

So Summer the plumber and Marky the Sparky,
were joking and chatting their usual malarkey.

When Saad came and asked if they had any clue,
If they saw the lunch and if anyone knew.

"It's good to ketchup and let's taco about it,
We doughnut know really you butter not doubt it!"

So lettuce see what the pear did here since ate,
"I sautéed the leeks and he fixed a switch plate."

Let's go speak to Shaina the expert dryliner,
Perhaps she can help out our famishing diner.

She's putting up walls made of plasterboard sheets,
On metal partitions, let's see what she eats.

"I don't have a lunch as my breakfast is big,
So is it that you mean to say I'm a pig?"

"No, who stole her lunch is just what we enquire,
Of course no suggestion that you are a liar."

Ty's coat buzzed as painters had radioed in,
As somebody there had knocked over a tin.

It made a big mess with the floor full of paint,
But that was not half the reason for complaint.

They felt as though someone had taken a brush,
And dipped it in paint then made off in a rush.

No brushes were missing but they found a trail,
'The paint will lead us to the thief without fail.'

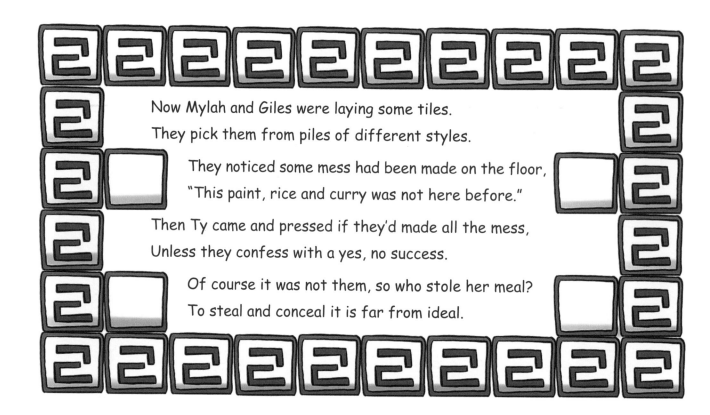

Now Mylah and Giles were laying some tiles.
They pick them from piles of different styles.

They noticed some mess had been made on the floor,
"This paint, rice and curry was not here before."

Then Ty came and pressed if they'd made all the mess,
Unless they confess with a yes, no success.

Of course it was not them, so who stole her meal?
To steal and conceal it is far from ideal.

When Ramaa and Harold were out on the scaffold,
They saw something striking that left them both baffled.

They put down their tubes and their boards and the clamp,
Untying their harness they walked to the ramp.

They saw blobs of paint with some pink and some white,
And strawberries while they were working at height.

The strawberry mess led on through to a door,
With more on the floor just before the big store.

The store room was always kept tidy and neat,
But what are these marks on this plasterboard sheet?

And who has knocked over this box and this crate,
This room was not left in this terrible state.

As John was patrolling when he heard a sound,
He could not believe it what he had just found.

A noise of a crunch and a munch from a box,
Uncovered the lunch thief and it was a fox!

UP

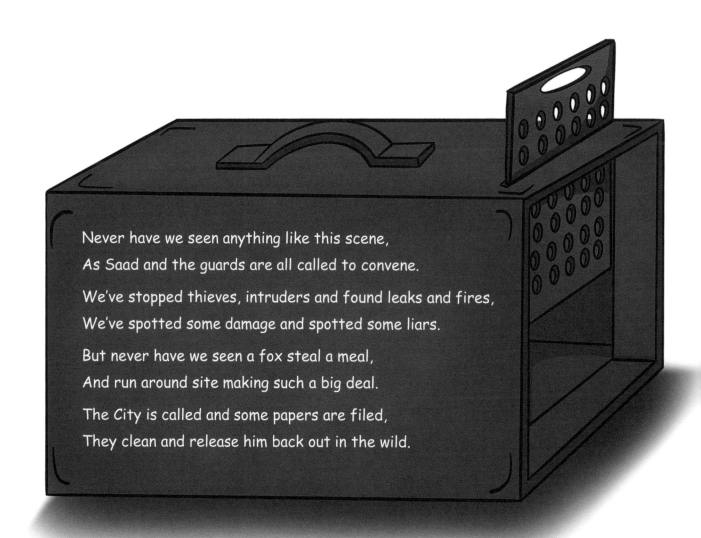

Never have we seen anything like this scene,
As Saad and the guards are all called to convene.

We've stopped thieves, intruders and found leaks and fires,
We've spotted some damage and spotted some liars.

But never have we seen a fox steal a meal,
And run around site making such a big deal.

The City is called and some papers are filed,
They clean and release him back out in the wild.

Now Ty had a thought as the thief had been caught,
Let's share with Miss Hayer the lunch that we brought.

So him and his team all sat in the canteen,
They put on display such a diverse cuisine.

Including Miss Hayer was such a nice touch,
She tried all the food and she ate way too much!

Miss Hayer was no longer sad with the theft,
And even the boss came across for what's left.

About this story (spoiler alert)

Based on the true story of 'Romeo' the fox, who was discovered on the 72nd floor of The Shard, whilst still under construction in 2011. Romeo had spent two weeks surviving on scraps of food left by builders before being found and taken to a nearby Animal Centre. He was subsequently released back onto the streets of Bermondsey.

Two years later, Romeo was immortalised, being the subject of a wooden monolith installed in the Grizedale Forest in Cumbria.

All profits from the sales of this book go to projects supporting local communities and construction related charities.